Immortal Bite

A DARK PARANORMAL ROMANCE NOVELLA

ANDIE M. LONG

Warning

This book contains mention of self-harm.

Should you be affected by any of the issues in this storyline, please see your G.P. or contact MIND.

To the darker part of myself.

At times you cause me pain; but you also give me a deeper understanding of the pleasures of life, and of the importance of feeling blessed every single day, no matter what.

One

VIVIENNE

Blood dripped from my thumb. Crimson red; just one small ruby tear escaping where I pulled out the thorn. I felt our reaction bone deep, as that one infinitesimal bead vacated my skin and dropped to the ground. It splashed on the bare earth around the rose bush like an atomic bomb. My breath hitched, waiting... wondering what the fallout would be.

Our?

'Our' reaction?

Who stood with me?

Every time I woke from the dream it was the same. Vivid memories of rose bushes of all shapes, sizes, and species, and it always stopped when the thorn entered my skin and I bled. I could see the house; I could see the grounds; I could not see who kept me company. But I could *feel* them. Their presence always oh so close.

I lay in bed and stared at the ceiling of my warehouse apartment, trying to find images in the concrete. Rain dashed against the large floor-to-ceiling window of my bedroom, and I welcomed the angry lashing.

Come on, mother nature, show me what you've got. Is this the best you can do?

The rhythmic patter engulfed me like a lover teasing me to orgasm as I heard it build and subside, build and subside, until the sound ceased as the downpour ended.

Dragging myself to my feet, I wrapped up in my silk robe that had seen better days and padded on the concrete floor over to the window, mindful not to trip on my Aztec rug on my way. Fucking thing. I'd bought it because it was fashionable for warehouse living, and I'd kept it to punish myself for being a victim of commercialism.

Standing at the window, I couldn't care less that my robe had fallen open and one breast and half of my pubic hair was exposed to the street. The rain still dripping down my window offered me a disguise and to be bothered I'd have to feel things and most of the time I did not.

Not until the roses called to me.

I heard their whisper in my mind from my dreams: *show me, find me, feel me, let me* and like a sleepwalker I left the window and walked out of my room and into my studio.

I didn't drink. I didn't eat. I just painted.

When I was finished, the red paint from the rose petals and the browns of the stems covered my robe and my skin. It looked like old and new blood decorating me.

The cravings began.

Bathroom. Razor blades. Skin.

The cuts I made stung and I welcomed the pain. Not too deep; just a scratch really. I didn't actually want to kill myself today. At times it was tempting to search for the place where it all ended, to call time on the nothing, the dark empty void within me. The truth was I wanted to live, feel, experience; but the black ghost dog that followed me everywhere was a bossy beast and after I painted, after I cut, I just 'was' while it gave a victorious howl that I was closer to its bidding than I was freedom from its snapping jaw. I'd succumbed before and they'd locked me in a building as dark and empty as I, where they'd medicated me until I convinced them I was better.

Sometimes I stared at ceilings for hours. To outsiders they'd assume I lived a normal life as they witnessed me shopping, conversing, existing. But once I was back home and the door was firmly closed, I had to shower off the people I'd met; required silence to obliterate the incessant chatter of the ones I'd had to talk to.

People made me feel like ants were crawling over my skin.

Like they were consuming me from the outside in.

Scratching at my skin helped to eradicate them.

Maybe it was the scratches and the blood that made me dream of roses?

Maybe it was the hope that one day I would wake and *feel*, that made me dream of another?

Maybe it was the fact that dreams were better than my reality that called me to bed for hour upon hour upon hour.

I lived my life in greys.

And dreamed in vivid red.

Once more, I crossed the stone bridge that led me to the medieval manor with its grand turrets. But while the building should fascinate me, it affected me no more than seeing a reality show contestant. I wasn't interested in exteriors. Exteriors could mislead. Good people could be bad people and cheery folk could be the saddest people on earth.

I reached the end of the bridge and my mind told me to turn back; that once I stepped off the bridge my path was chosen, but my intuition told me this was where I needed to be.

That my life began here.

The rose bush at the end of the stone bridge was withered and dead. No more than twigs and the dry husks of unopened buds.

Your death is here.

Your life is here.

More whispers came into my mind from the roses. I followed their murmurs on the wind, stepped off the bridge and walked past the decaying rose bush. The enormous vista of the manor with its many windows stood before me, but I followed the whisperings all the way to the back of the building, to the gardens. A large stone seat was positioned where I could sit and see the garden; but for some reason, I knew deep within that the garden couldn't see me. It felt me, but it couldn't see me. Not yet.

Come. Step inside. Touch me. Let me.

Rising, I entered the garden and I walked towards

the smallest rose. Unassuming and the red of pillar boxes, I reached to touch a petal and its softness warmed my skin.

See, you are <u>feeling</u>.

I was. I was. My face ached as a smile appeared upon it, as rare as a white peacock. It was foreign, but I felt that maybe it could stay awhile.

Touch me, take me. I can remind you of how to <u>feel</u>.

I went to pluck the rose and there it was.

The thorn in my thumb.

The crimson bead.

And I felt him behind me. The other part of the 'our'.

I took the path and now it was fated.

This is where it began, and ended, and began again.

I heard him speak.

"Welcome to Tetburn Manor."

Two

CALEB

My turning was violent and without consent.

But I survived; if the life I led now could be called that.

I was *lucky*. The word hit my mind and made me laugh, an unamused huff. My beloved fiancé of the time was not. She was drained and cast aside in front of my eyes, before my sire was slain and my saviour, Nicholas of Turrim Londoniarium clan, took me in and taught me how to be a vampire that could exist in the world without harming another.

He gave me Tetburn Manor and staff who would ask no questions. Staff who had their own secrets and reasons for being there. Some were vampire, some were human. They kept themselves largely apart and did their tasks, including collecting donated human blood for me to drink, given by those who found it a thrill or a profitable career; and helping me run my business.

I cared for and sold roses.

My tribute to Rosemary Lyons, my never-to-be wife. I made sure that as I lived on, so did her memory.

But as almost one hundred years had passed, my memories of her had faded away; and the importance of tending the roses and ensuring *their* survival had become an obsession.

———

"Caleb, have you finished with your drink?" Daria, my house manager hovered in the doorway. My dining hall was rectangular and vast: twice as long as it was wide, twice as high as it was wide, and with large windows to one side that looked over the front of my home, or should that be my *manor*. From here I could see the front lawns, the gravel paths, and the stone bridges that led to the outside world. There were security gates and fences to keep that outside world out unless I wished it otherwise.

In the olden days, Daria would have entered through the screens passage at the rear of the room, but now we had modernised and she'd enter through a nearer doorway connecting the modern kitchen to this room. She was still some distance away from me now, but she knew my vampire hearing meant I'd heard every word.

I picked up my 'drink', my daily glass of O-negative that stopped me from wanting to kill the human staff. I didn't need to drink the whole thing daily, but I did anyway. I never wanted to leave even the remotest chance of a replay of how I myself was sired. How my love was destroyed with a fanged bite, torn apart. I finished, wiping my mouth on the white linen napkin. A faint crimson stain decorated it like fresh raspberries dyed my china plates. Food had no nutritional value, but my enhanced senses meant their taste was divine. I had a corner of the kitchen garden set up for raspberry growing. Maybe it was the fact their colour was like my most favoured roses and their canes had the same sharp thorns?

Daria came over and took the empty glass from my proffered hand.

"Thank you."

"So what's on today's agenda, Sir?" She asked, a hint of a smirk at her lip.

"I think I shall spend some time in my office on paperwork and orders and then I shall possibly go care for my roses." I returned her smile. My day never changed from its same routine and while some might find it wearisome, for me I welcomed the familiar and the ordinary. It was a good life and a safe life. I gave to the world the beauty of nature and in return it gave me peace.

"And what about you, Daria? How shall you spend your day?"

"Well, Sir. I think I shall oversee that everyone is doing what they should be and then I will probably be at the vegetable and fruit borders, doing maintenance and procuring some ready crops for the evening dinner. Lucinda is after cooking all of us a vegetable stew this evening, so I'd better hope I don't disappoint her."

Tetburn Manor had a daily routine and I welcomed it.

Our cook, Lucinda, was amazing at putting dishes together. She kept the staff fed and happy and knew how to make my vampire tastebuds zing with delight. She was a treasure.

"Yes, you make sure to keep Lucinda happy."

"I will, Sir." She smiled.

Daria left the dining hall and went to join the rest of the staff in keeping the manor in order, and I rose from my seat. Though I could have been in my office in a blink of a human eye, I took my time, gazing at the familiar architecture: the timbered ceilings, high windows, the stone staircase. There were formal paintings on the walls of forebears that weren't mine but held severe faces that felt like they were keeping watch on the building. Reaching the top of the stairs, I walked down the landing until I reached the door of my office. Pushing the heavy iron key in the lock and turning until I heard the familiar 'click', I opened the large wooden door, hearing its recognizable creak. Stepping inside, I walked straight over to the window where I pulled back the shutters revealing the outside. A protective layer was fixed to all the windows that obscured the sunlight from entering the manor. It meant that when I rose at around 4pm, the summer sunlight could not burn my skin.

Though I'd been born in 1889 and turned in 1921, I had moved with the times and anyone who met me would think I was born of the era of smartphones, WiFi, and Converse. I wore my dark hair short but styled with paste, and I dressed mainly in jeans and various different coloured t-shirts. Though my skin was cold to the touch, I myself was always an optimal body temperature and had no need of a sweater outdoors.

Laptop powered up, I cleared the pending emails and reviewed the orders, printing out a list of what I needed to ensure was done today. Opening my mail, I had a cursory glance at the sample catalogue for the next season and found it lacking. It needed something to make it stand out in a sea of competitors, but what I didn't know.

I noticed I was restless. Something I'd not experienced in a long, long time. Why? Looking around my plain office with its bureau, chairs, chaise longue, and walls with photos of my favourite roses, I felt unsettled in my own skin. Like today this usual life wasn't suiting me. It was as if I'd changed detergent and my skin was itching and desperate to escape my clothing. Maybe I shouldn't have drunk the O-neg. It was possible that because my levels weren't low that I'd overdone it. Once more, I stood and gazed out of the window. I'd get myself out in the garden earlier than usual and work off some energy. Hopefully then I would feel more myself.

From seemingly nowhere, a wave of agony washed over me and I clutched at my chest. *What the hell was happening?* Tremors wracked my body and I clutched the window ledge. A cold sweat began to cover my body, drops of liquid running down my face, dripping from my chin. I could feel it running between my pecs. I swiped my hand underneath my t-shirt to stop the almost tickle.

And then I staggered some more, all the way back to my leather office chair where I fell upon it with a thud, as I took in a similar sensation beneath my hand.

Th-thud.

Th-thud.

Th-thud.

My undead heart had started beating.

My hand hovered away from my flesh, but I could still hear it pulsing in my ears.

Th-thud

Th-thud

Th-thud.

I'd been told of a beating heart by Nicholas and had dismissed his teachings with derision. For I knew what he said caused such a phenomenon and knew that it would never knock at my door.

A newly beating heart meant that my mate was here.

My love.

So had ghosts risen from my past with Rosemary, or was love destined to bloom from elsewhere?

I sat with my hand upon my beating heart for so long, that Daria came to see why I'd not reached the gardens on time.

Change was in the air. You could almost taste it.

Three

VIVIENNE

For once I was out of my bed with intent and purpose and no delay. Not bothering to clothe myself, I stumbled into the living room, grabbed my laptop and trailed back into my bedroom where I crawled back under the covers. It took its usual seemingly never-ending time to open properly. My mind reminded me that its capacity was struggling under the weight of my downloads, and that I kept promising to clear it. It was an empty promise, much like the ones my family made to me. The ones still alive, that was.

'We'll come see you soon'.

No, you won't. Because you'll be reminded that I'm not whole and you don't want to deal with the pieces. Scared that by being in my company, my illness may mutate and infect you.

Google appeared on my screen. I typed 'Tetburn Manor' into the search bar and then I gasped, peering closer at the screen. Because there it was. The house from my dreams.

Clicking onto a Wikipedia page that I knew could be full of half-truths, I poured over the words, photos, and illustrations.

The photo showed me the grand façade of the house, but I really didn't need to look at it very closely because I already knew every part of its outer shell: every brick, every turret, every gravelled path. The layout of its gardens. It was the inside I knew nothing about at all.

I discovered the house was built in the 15th Century and was home to the Brown family until the early 19th century when an unnamed organisation took over its ownership. For the past one hundred years the house had been noted for its roses, grown by the Miller family. Cloaked in secrecy, not much was known about the Miller family other than the rose business grew from strength to strength under the current watchful gaze of a Caleb Miller, current CEO of Tetburn Roses.

Opening another tab, I typed in his name in order that I might see a photograph of someone who could be part of my 'our', but there was nothing. I was left dissatisfied, like a lover had walked out on me as I was on the cusp of coming, or the needle had been pulled from my arm just before the drugs hit my system.

A hunger like I'd not eaten for days gnawed at me as I went back to the description and looked for the address.

Eynsford, Kent.

Pushing the laptop to one side, I dragged out some clothes from the floor, sniffing them and putting them on. A pair of ripped black skinny jeans, a red t-shirt, a black hoody. Kate Spade pumps would be the only 'tell' to fellow Tube and rail travellers that I wasn't some junkie out looking for a fix. My reflection showed my pale face with its hollowed cheekbones, and dark shadows under my dead-looking eyes. I pulled my greasy looking hair into a ponytail, and grabbed my essentials, plus my sketchpad and pencils.

Travelling on the Circle Line, I stared between

heads watching nothing in particular. Most passengers ignored me, but I could feel the judgy stares of the others. How they held their handbags closer to their chest because they felt I might covet what they had. If I let myself I would, but it wouldn't be the contents of their handbags. I would want to steal the looks that passed between them and their loved ones, their excitement at wherever they were headed. I had money. It fed my body, but never my soul.

I pulled at my sleeves often, ensuring they didn't ride up. Didn't show my wounds any more than my face did. People couldn't read pain and sorrow. It was much easier for them to dismiss someone as a junkie or an alcoholic or a bum. Then they could step back, dismiss. Consciences couldn't do that if they saw misery and despair. Then they'd feel a need to step in, and no one really wanted to do that. They just wanted an easy life. I couldn't blame them, and I wouldn't want anyone's help anyway. I'd already told you that people made my skin itch. Their help would make me bleed, literally.

From the Tube station, I walked and caught a train at Blackfriars where I had to sit for another fifty-five minutes until I finally reached Eynsford.

Off the train, I had an approximate twenty-minute walk to the stone bridge if my Google Maps was correct. Given how spectacularly I usually managed to fuck up reading it, it was unsurprising when it took me closer to forty-five minutes to get to the edge of the manor. Wooden and barbed wire fencing surrounded the estate, but I had anticipated it would. I took the bolt cutters from my backpack and made an opening at the edge of the estate where woodland met wildflower meadow met unruly untended fields. I continued walking the periphery until I saw the stone bridge.

This would do for today. I sat amongst the overgrowth, took out my pad and pencils and sketched until the light had left the sky.

I knew I needed to get up and go home, but my body felt quiet for the first time in a long time. My mind was not overrun with thoughts and I could feel the tickle of the grass. The insects here would bite me if I stayed, but I didn't want to leave.

From the photographs, I knew that some of the supports of the stone bridge jutted out of flowerbeds. It was a place I could put down my backpack as a pillow and pull my hoody tighter around me. The evening was not cold, and this area escaped the rain. If I slept here, even for just a few hours, then I could sketch again when the sun rose. I had a flask of cold coffee and snacks.

Mind made up. I moved over to the bridge and I laid in its shadow and slept until sunrise.

When I awoke, for a moment I panicked, wondering where I was. My neck was stiff and so my first thought was that I'd fallen asleep in the studio. It wouldn't be the first time I'd hurt myself doing so. But the bright light hit my face and I remembered I was lying in the flowerbed near the bridge.

Shit! What had I been thinking? People would use this bridge to get to the manor, wouldn't they? Tentatively, I looked up to see if there was anyone peering down at the strange woman lying in the soil, but there was nothing. I could hear noise and the hum of an engine, but it wasn't close, and I just knew without knowing how, that there were two stone bridges, more or less side by side; identical in every way, except one was used and one was not.

Sitting up, I took out my ponytail, shook my head, and ran my hands through my pale-blonde hair in case any spiders or other creatures had decided to live there overnight. Then I tied it back up. I moved back to the place I sketched yesterday, relieving myself behind a tree first, and I drank some now rank coffee and eagerly ate a KitKat.

I was obsessed with my work and I stayed there for hours. Occasionally, I leant against a tree and snoozed for an hour, but then I was back at it, sketching page after page.

My craving started, but this time it was not for razor blades.

Come closer. Closer than this. See me. Feel me. Hear me. Touch me.

Gathering my belongings, I walked back to the stone bridge but this time right around to where I could step onto it.

I shouldn't do this.

What if I was caught?

I was now clearly trespassing on private property.

Well, they should have ensured their boundaries were more secure.

Anyway, I only wanted to paint. Their valuables were worthless to me, my yearning only for a naturally discarded petal.

I walked the whole length of the stone bridge and no one stopped me. As I reached the end, I saw the rose bush from my dreams, but it was not dead, not withered. Not in the slightest. It bloomed, but the petals were yellow, and it was covered in greenfly.

This rose was me right now, and I knew its future.

Dead.

Withered.

Uncared for.

Unless someone stepped in to save it.

I sat next to it and began to draw.

The sound of voices startled me, and I slipped back into the shadow of the huge bridge.

What the fuck had I been thinking?

As soon as the coast appeared clear, I made my way off the bridge, through the land and back to public transport.

I was given even sourer looks and wider berths given that I was now covered in dirt, smelled of body odour, and possibly had even half-peed down myself. It's not like I had a lot of practice of urinating in bushes.

I didn't care. All I wanted to do was to get home and get in my studio.

And that's what I did. Once through the door, I painted and sketched, painted and sketched. But it wasn't enough. The dreams told me so, when I took the time to close my eyes.

You didn't come to us.

We need you.

Come back.

I woke knowing that my lips just uttered 'yes' on the edge of waking.

Four

CALEB

When Daria brought me my blood the next day, her hand went to her throat.

"Sir, can I hear…?"

"My beating heart? It would appear so." I scratched at my head.

"I do not understand it, Daria. I, of course, know about finding one's mate and it starting the beat of a vampire's heart, but nothing has changed. Yesterday was exactly the same as any other day."

A cautious smile broke out on her face and she reached out and gently tapped my shoulder before removing her hand.

"Something must have changed somewhere. With a gesture, or a thought, at some point during your day, the fates aligned, and you found your mate."

I noted Daria was far more excited about this than I was.

"I shall go to see Nicholas at some point. See if he has heard of this phenomenon happening in other instances."

Daria nodded. "Well, Sir, I shall leave you to your drink and your ponderings. I shall no doubt see you in the garden later while I tend the vegetables and you tend the roses. Good afternoon, Sir."

"Good afternoon, Daria. I hope the sun shone on the crops today."

"I hope its warmth caused your roses to bloom."

I smiled up at her, cheered by the chatter of my beloved garden. "How amusing that we welcome the sun on our gardens, given the damage it can do to us while we slumber."

"Very true, Sir. Very true."

With that Daria left.

It wasn't long before I was interrupted, something that rarely happened during my first mealtime after waking and usually meant an urgent matter.

I immediately tensed as my main security officer, Jenson, walked into the room.

"Sir, the perimeter alarms went off late last night. It would appear we had a visitor. Looks like maybe a homeless person. Would you be able to come and see?"

I nodded and rose to follow him.

My instructions on intruders were clear; unless they caused harm or crossed the outer walls of the property, they were to be left until I had checked the security footage. My estate was vast enough and secure enough that if someone wanted to camp outside for one night, it didn't hurt to let them.

I watched as the intruder, a small dot on the screen, made their way over to the stone bridge and then settled there. No harm, no foul. I was disinterested. It looked like a youth, given the hoody.

"They then got braver," Jenson explained as the screen changed to show different footage. Now daytime, it was clear to see as the woman walked up the bridge getting nearer and nearer until she reached the rose bush that stood halfway between the bridge and the wall of my property. Fascinated, I watched the screen as the woman fell to her knees and began sketching. After a while, I saw her startle and look over more in the direction of the main house, then she turned and left.

"So, she just sketched?"

"It would appear so, Sir. It's a strange one, to come all this way to draw a rose bush. No disrespect, Sir, I know they're our business, but I'm sure she could have gone to a garden centre or somewhere a lot nearer. I can't help but feel suspicious. Why did she come here?"

His question set off something in my brain. It was like my synapses snapped together.

Why did she come here?

"Can you zoom in on her? I doubt I know her, but we should make a note of what she looks like in case she returns."

"Good idea. Shame she didn't leave a self-portrait behind, hey, Sir?" Jenson quipped.

"Indeed." I humoured him. He was a nice man and loyal, given he was human and served a vampire.

As he zoomed in, her features became more apparent. Lank hair, dark shadowed eyes, and the cut-glass cheekbones of the malnourished.

"Definitely looks like an addict, or a homeless person. Perhaps painting gets them money?"

I shrugged my shoulders. "Who knows? Let me know if you see her again." I watched as she walked back down the bridge and away, and I noticed a small piece of paper left her pile and fluttered away in the breeze.

After dealing with things in my office, I made my way towards the rose garden, but just as I almost reached there, thoughts of the wayward paper hit me. I should go see if I could find it.

My mind ridiculed my thoughts. *As if that will still be around. It will have blown into the lake by now.*

Spotting Daria in the vegetable garden, I smiled and carried on past, noting first her look of pleasure at seeing me, and then her look of confusion, her forehead creasing as I turned and walked in a different direction.

She ran after me.

"Is everything okay, Sir?"

"Yes, Daria. Don't mind me. I don't want to upset the dinner routine. I just fancy a stroll down the East Bridge. It's been a while."

"You sure you don't want company?"

I waved her off with my hand. "No, I'm fine."

I walked out of the walled gardens, across the fine gravel pathway and reached the rose bush where I noted its greenfly.

"I shall be back to attend to you, dear one. You

may not be one of my prize roses, but you are family nonetheless."

Then I passed around it and started my walk down the bridge.

At the end of the bridge, I stepped down into the overgrown grass and saw where it had been trampled by recent footsteps. Without really thinking about it too much I followed the trampled grass. My visitor had been under the stone bridge and also in the edge of the woodland, but she had left no other trace than trampled ground and her scent.

Coming back to the reality of the day, I decided to head back to the gardens to tend to my dear roses, and then I saw it. A white piece of something, billowing slightly from where it was stuck in a shrub, like a large Cabbage White butterfly on brassicas.

When I reached it, I plucked it from the bush and then gasped as the pain hit me again.

Th-thud

Th-thud

Th-thud.

My eyes alighted on the paper, a small drawing of a rose and then doodled words.

Come to me.

Touch me.

Taste me.

Feel me.

My cock stirred and my heart beat so hard in my chest, I thought it would burst from its cavity.

I now knew what had caused my heart to beat again.

The mystery artist.

But what had brought her to Tetburn Manor?

Was she a vampire?

Or... human.

How could she be my mate?

What was her name? I turned the paper and searched for an artist's signature but found nothing.

Disappointed, I dropped to my knees, dropped the paper, and surrendered to the pain in my body.

Five

VIVIENNE

I painted all through the night, but now my artwork was not only of roses. I sketched the bridge, I sketched the manor, I sketched a shadow man. Just a black silhouette. I had no idea how I knew his height, his frame, but I drew him in the periphery of the manor or at the window.

My dreams stopped speaking to me, or maybe it was my complete exhaustion. That morning I awoke and I felt... calm.

The peace I felt was only usually experienced for brief blissful moments after cutting and so I laid there, staring at my ceiling, drinking in the contentment that currently blessed my body. I waited for it to leave me, but it remained.

Practically leaping out of bed, I pulled upon the curtains revealing a bright, sunny day and I opened the windows, letting in the fresh air. I took a deep inhale, annoyed to smell the fumes of London instead of the air of the countryside. Turning back to my room, I glanced around, taking in the complete and utter mess and devastation. Paint was smeared on the bedding, the floors. I looked down at myself. Yes, I was covered too. Discarded clothes littered the floor. My footprints trailed out of the door, no doubt all the way to the studio, maybe to the kitchen.

I felt the urge to clean, starting with myself. I grabbed a shower, and then dressed in clean clothes. I left the house to grab a coffee, food, more painting supplies, and cleaning materials.

Sat in the coffee shop nursing an Americano after a quick hit of an espresso, I took a bite from my bacon sandwich and took in its flavour.

"You have a little ketchup running from your lip," another customer, sitting at the next table pointed out. Usually, I would have scowled, wiped my mouth and thought 'mind your own fucking business', but today I smiled, thanked them and licked the sauce from my lip as if it were blood dripping from the mouth of a vampire. Mmm, except blood wasn't bursting with fruity flavours. I'd smelled mine, tasted it as I licked up my cuts to make them smart more. Sometimes I'd poured whisky down my throat and then into the scratches.

I'd looked at my arms as I'd showered. Faint scarring showed, but my latest cuts were scabbed and healing. The lack of fresh ones was unusual. I felt *unusual*.

Numb. Black. Despondent. Bleak. That was my *normal*.

I had no idea how to describe what was happening to me right now. Even as a child I'd been melancholic.

Somehow, I just knew it was all connected to Tetburn Manor. Even thinking of the place made my heart soar. Was that... joy?

I left the coffee shop, even saying goodbye to the person who'd been sitting at the next table and to the serving staff. I walked to the art shop and stocked up on the paint I'd run out of, and then I bought white spirit and other cleaning things and returned to the apartment.

By the time I collapsed into my bed that night, exhausted, the warehouse was clean. The vast living room smelled of freshly laundered clothes as I laid them out over every available surface to dry. My paintings were stacked in a pile and fresh canvases were out ready. Only one painting had been moved, hung on the wall above my bed.

A watercolour of Tetburn Manor, set in a border of roses, with a shadow man at one window.

And a new rug laid at my feet. No longer would I be punished by Aztec prints. I'd been back out to the shops, frustrated that I couldn't carry everything I'd wanted, and a rose-petal design rug now covered the space at the side of my bed.

My bliss lasted barely twenty-four more hours.

After breakfast I walked to my nearest park and yanked off all the rose heads before the park ranger told me to fuck off.

Back in my flat, I pulled off the petals one by one and threw them on the floor so that everywhere I walked, I walked among their fragrance, their colour. I could feel my own fading. The pinks of the petals began to fade, drying and curling up at the edges becoming oranges and browns, and I could no longer smell them. My mind was full of death and decay and I swore I could smell bare earth, like it was waiting for my rotting corpse.

I closed my bedroom curtains, blocking out the day, and I laid down in my freshly made bed and I cried. Sobs wracked my body until the numbness returned and my bedroom once again became my prison.

And so I closed my eyes to sleep, because it was the only way to escape.

"Who are you?" The voice came from behind me. From behind the stone bench.

"I'm Vivienne."

*"Yes, but **who are you**? As in why are you here? Why do you keep visiting my manor, my garden?"*

"I don't know. I just need to be here."

"But why?"

"Because it's the only place I feel alive."

*The dream moved on and I was standing **inside** the manor in a room with bare white walls. Yet, instead of feeling the peace I got from Tetburn, here my heart was gripped with fear as I turned around and around, seeing nothing but the white.*

And then there was pain.

I most certainly was not numb here.

The pain at my throat was excruciating and

bright red blood sprayed out and coated the bare white wall in front of me.

I looked down at my white gown. It looked like I'd spilled red wine, but I knew it wasn't wine at all.

The door opened and the shadow man was there. I could feel his presence.

I turned around and I saw his teeth.

Large incisors as white as the walls.

And I saw his eyes.

As red as the blood spraying from my throat.

And I heard his heart beating.

Th-thud.

Th-thud.

Th-thud.

As I knew my own was ceasing.

I woke, clutching at my throat. I switched on my light and looked at my hand as I trembled. Red coated my hand and I felt sick.

Stumbling out of bed, I dry heaved, as panic filled my system.

It was a dream. How could I have been injured?

As I woke properly, I realised that my hand was covered in paint and I saw that once again paint trailed from my room.

I followed it all the way to the studio where gasping I looked at the fresh canvasses I'd left.

Every one was laid around the room, bright red paint thrown at them like the blood of a slaughtered animal on snow.

I'd sleepwalked and painted?

And then dreamed?

I sat amongst the paintings and put my head in my hands. Confusion gave me a tension headache. At least I was feeling something, I guessed.

I checked in with myself.

What was I feeling?

Panic.

Disorientation.

Cravings.

But not for my blades. Once again, I craved the house with the roses, and the shadow man. Today, I would shop again. For a camping trip. I was returning to Tetburn Manor and this time I wasn't leaving until I got answers to the questions of my dreams.

The roses wanted me?

I was coming for them.

CALEB

The pain in my body had ceased.

The torment in my mind had increased.

A day passed and there was no sign of the intruder again. My heart still beat but it was slower, and I wondered if one day I would wake to find it had stopped once more.

Frustrated, I decided to go visit my clan leader to find out more about mates and beating hearts.

I did not know how unusual my plans were until my staff stared at me in shock. It would have been amusing were it not for the fact I wanted to get out of there and not be delayed by having to explain myself.

"But, Sir, you have not left the manor in over fifty years." Daria's brow creased.

Jenson nodded his head. "You haven't left the whole time I have worked here. I'd bet my father would corroborate Daria's timeline."

It wasn't something I'd considered. Years sped by when you were immortal and living a life of routine.

"Well there's no need for panic. I'm only visiting Nicholas, not joining the circus."

"But we will worry about you when you're gone." Daria's bottom lip trembled.

"Daria, dear, throw a party while the Lord of the Manor is away." I laughed at her. "I'm only going out for a couple of hours. I should imagine I'll be back by ten at the latest."

I put on my coat and stood at the entrance waiting for one of the clan drivers to come to pick me up. "Maybe we are in too much of a mundane routine here at Tetburn Manor. Perhaps we do need to change things up a little?"

Lights began to creep up the West Bridge and with one last look at their wide-eyed expressions, I laughed and went to meet it.

Nicholas had taken me in after my sire had been slain just after my turning by a vampire he'd wronged. I'd been feral and vengeful and had slaughtered my sire's small clan with the assistance of the rogue vampire. Captured by one of the Turrim Londoniarium clan, they'd brought me to Nicholas' lair where he'd cared for me until I was able to stand on my own two feet. My payment had been to tend to his private gardens, something I'd found joy in. Something that quieted my tortured mind.

And then he'd given me Tetburn Manor to live in, and my own gardens to tend; helping me track down different cultivars of roses until my beloved collection thrived where my past love could not. I'd learned to breed my own varieties and started the business. Roses not only reminded me of her name, but the petals reflected the fragility of life: the thorns life's evil stab, often experienced unwittingly. And as I watched red buds bloom and thorns scratch at my skin, leaving not a blemish, they reminded me of my true nature. The vampire: with a thirst for blood and with the thorny sting of canines.

"Caleb, my man. It takes a lot to shock a vampire as old as I, but when they said you wanted to visit, I have to admit I panicked. You're one of the clan I consider most settled."

I shook Nicholas' hand and followed him through to his study. The tall blonde man sat and pointed to the chair opposite him.

"So, your heart began beating, but you've no idea why?" He tilted his head and gestured with a hand for me to speak.

"I have no firm evidence of why it would start."

"You haven't met anyone new? Developed feelings for any of the staff?"

"God, no. My staff are valued, but I don't have anything but a general fondness for their loyalty to me. And I haven't met anyone new..." My voice trailed off.

Nicholas raised a brow. "But...?"

I scrubbed a hand through my hair. "We had a woman camp out on the grounds for a night. She came up to the front of the East Bridge. The security cameras revealed her to be sketching a rose bush. She looked like she was maybe homeless or an addict. Then she left, and she hasn't returned." I licked my lip. "My heart began beating that very same day. I went out into the gardens to find a piece of paper she'd dropped and when I put my hands upon it, my heart thudded so hard, my body wracked with pain, and I fell to my knees."

Nicholas' lips curved. "Then I do believe we have found who your mate is, my friend."

"But I have never seen her before in my life, and possibly will never see her again."

Nicholas shook his head. "If she is indeed your mate then she will be back. You will call to her. Your very essence shall sing through the wind all the way to her open window. Mates cannot be denied. The connection is too strong."

"You believe she will return?"

"I know she will. Now, tell me more about her and let's catch up on what you've been up to for the last few decades, shall we? How are my roses doing?"

After leaving Nicholas and returning to my home, I wandered the house and gardens for a while, looking at them with fresh eyes. I went into the nurseries and checked on the new roses. It took years for us to release a new 'cross', taking the best of other roses and transferring the pollen from one plant to another, collecting hips and then sowing the seed. We then watched the seedlings. From thousands of these plants we might end up with half a dozen new varieties. But as time meant relatively little to an immortal, what did it matter that it took so long?

The human staff who worked here had forebears that had worked here for generations. We needed human staff for selling and marketing purposes. You couldn't run a business selling flowers where there was no one to show them in the sunlight. They were all trusted by the clan and valuable assets to Tetburn Manor.

Daria sought me out. "The wanderer returns and is now wandering about his own manor like a first-time visitor. Are you okay, Sir? I am worried about you."

I smiled at her. "Well, instead of worrying, come join me."

She looked hesitant.

"I promise I've not gone crazy; you'll be perfectly safe with me."

"I know. I trust you. But I'm staff. What will people say if they see me walking around the manor with you?"

I shrugged my shoulders. "Then grab a paper and pen. For I think we are going to change a few things around here. It's been a while since we had any new refurbishments and I want something new to look at."

Daria rushed over to a bureau, grabbed a pen and paper and ran to catch me up.

"The thing is, Daria. Being immortal, as we are, means we sometimes get in a rut. Time passes, so much time, and we don't notice as much as our human employees. The interior of here is dated and the outside has huge potential. Let us make plans!"

Enthused, I went around, chatting about changing the old severe-looking artwork, painting the walls with fresh paint. Then outside, I discussed changing the overgrown land near the East Bridge, making it a nature sanctuary and a wildflower meadow. All the time I walked around, I was looking through the eyes of what I expected an artist would like. Clear white walls on which to hang fresh paintings. A meadow teeming with different colours and varieties of flowers to choose from. Did she also sculpt? She could make statues and other things perhaps? My mind ran on and on.

"Well, Sir, I feel you have quite the list. Shall we review it tomorrow and then we can discuss you talking to Nicholas about getting trusted craftspeople to make some of the changes?"

"Perhaps. For now, I think I shall be satisfied

with mulling things over further. Thank you for taking notes, and for spending your evening with me and my ramblings."

"Not at all, Sir. It was most enjoyable. Good evening and I shall see you tomorrow."

I nodded my head at her, but barely noticed her leaving, such was my active mind. When would my artist come back? Was Nicholas right, that she'd not be able to stay away?

I found out my answer two days later, as Jenson interrupted my first drink of the day to tell me the intruder was back and had been painting the yellow roses once more. I smiled, as this time there were no greenfly to be seen. Would she notice and be pleased? Or would she be annoyed, preferring to see the natural order of things?

I played the security footage in my room, watching her walk up the bridge again and her kneeling in front of the rose. This time she looked different. Her hair was pale blonde and looked clean, though it was wrapped up in a messy knot on the top of her head. Still, zooming in, I could see that soft tendrils fell against her cheeks. She wore a white t-shirt and cut-off jean shorts, revealing long, tanned legs. As she painted, she became so entranced in her work that soon her clothes were covered in paint. Her face looked less haunted, and in fact the longer she painted, the more the creases appeared to fall from her brow and she looked at peace.

It was with regret that I saw her pack up her things and leave as the light began to fade. She was stopping at the point where I began. I would never be able to experience what she saw, the light casting its shadows and bringing out the best colours, but I could get her to paint and hang them in the manor. That way maybe she would bring some of that sunshine into the darkness of my home. My mystery artist bloomed in summer and I thrived in winter, but as I recalled the darkness and shadows upon her face, I realised that at times she lived in winter too. As my roses brought out the summer of my nature, it felt we were in some strange juxtaposition—somehow making a whole.

I scoffed at myself. I was spending too much of my time in fanciful thoughts. What was going on with me?

I tried to settle, to relax, but it was impossible. Finally, I got to my feet from my seat in the office and left the manor once more. I would go searching where she'd come from again and see if she'd left anymore pieces of paintings. I felt my heart beating but my body was now becoming accustomed to the rhythm. No longer feeling pain, I placed my hand on top of my chest and welcomed the feeling that I was waking up, becoming alive in a way I'd not experienced for a century.

As I dipped down from the East Bridge and walked again among the trampled down grass, I heard it.

Th-thud.

Th-thud.

Th-thud.

But this time it was not the beat of my own heart.

It was hers...

Seven

VIVIENNE

Once again, being in the vicinity of the manor and painting had made me feel more at ease with myself. I'd set up my small tent in the woodland and was pleased I could stay here for an extra amount of time, having brought more essentials with me on this occasion. After filling my tummy with a sandwich, and a bar of chocolate, I had drunk half a bottle of wine and now felt the sleepy elation usually assigned to the just-fucked.

A twig snapped nearby, and I quickly ducked behind a tree.

"I know you are here. You have nothing to worry

about. I don't mind. It's quite nice having an artist in residence."

It was *his* voice, the shadow man's.

Slowly, I came out from behind the tree, but I couldn't see him.

"Where are you?"

"I am keeping my distance so as not to alarm you."

"Why would you alarm me?" I was intrigued that he was hiding but tantalized at the same time. Delayed gratification could be *very* satisfying.

"That is a story for another day. For now, why not sit awhile outside your tent and I will stay here for just a moment."

"I'll stay standing if that's okay with you," I said curtly. "And I have a knife, so don't even think about jumping out at me. I'll gut you like a fish."

A chuckle drifted over to me. "Sounds fair, but I have no intention of coming any nearer. So tell me, why are you painting my roses and sleeping on my land?"

I hesitated. "I was just passing and have an inquisitive mind."

"I've watched you on my security videos. You lose yourself completely in your work. It is something to behold, but it seems a long way to come to paint a quite ordinary garden rose."

"I know little about roses, but I know this is Tetburn Manor and I doubt any of these roses are ordinary."

Another laugh. "Well, that one was here when I arrived, and I kept it, so I guess its ordinariness against a backdrop of special blooms makes it extraordinary in its own right."

I swallowed. "Would you like me to leave? Is that why you are here? You could have sent security to get rid of me, Caleb."

A small gasp sounded. "You know who I am and yet you haven't seen me. How?"

I shrugged my shoulders, though I had no idea whether he could see me do so or not. "I just do. It's hard to explain."

There was a moment of silence. "I would like to invite you to dinner. Tomorrow evening, 8pm? I would like to show you the rose garden, my prized collections. I have a business proposition for you. There is no need for you to be out here skulking about like a trespasser. My manor walls need paintings. Bring some of your recent work with you."

"I'll think about it," I replied, but I was talking to fresh air.

The shadow man had disappeared among the darkness, making barely a sound.

I tried to sleep after that, but it was impossible. If it weren't for the time of night I'd have made my way back to my own home to see what I could wear to dinner tomorrow, but instead, I drank the other half of the bottle of wine and dozed in my tent until first light broke. Then I packed my things and returned to my apartment because if this dinner went well, I'd not need to camp in secret again.

I settled on a long-sleeved pink silk shirt and my usual skinny black jeans. I added a long silver chain to add a little class to my outfit given I was wearing trainers on my feet. Well, he had told me we would be walking.

My mind wandered, thinking about why he'd kept to the shadows. Was it like The Phantom of the Opera? Was he monstrous? It was certainly possible. There were no photos of him in circulation after all. The mysterious rose grower. I placed a vegetable knife in my handbag just in case. Finally ready, with my art folio accompanying me, I returned once more to the manor. Even the constant travel on public transport couldn't pull down my mood tonight, and this time at the train station I caught a cab to Tetburn Manor and travelled up the West Bridge like a normal person.

A woman met me at the entrance. She looked my age, around thirty, and was attractive with long dark-brown hair and light-brown eyes. She was petite and slim, and I might have wondered if she was Caleb's wife had she not been wearing a suit, and a badge that declared her Daria Valente, House Manager.

She beamed at me and gestured inside. "Hello. I'm very grateful to make your acquaintance. I'm Daria. My apologies for my boss who didn't think to ask you what your own name was."

I laughed. I'd not even noticed. "My name is Vivienne. Vivienne Gladstone."

She held out a hand and I shook it.

"Pleased to meet you, Miss Gladstone. If you'd like to follow me." Her skin was cold to the touch, mine seeming sweaty in her palm.

Withdrawing my hand, I followed her down the hall. "Call me Vivienne, please."

"Okay. Thank you." I received another smile in return. "It has been years since Mr Miller had a dinner guest, so you must excuse us if we forget the proper etiquette this evening."

My smile slipped a little. Was I having dinner with a disfigured old man? Oh well, whatever it took to get me in those gardens.

This meant I wasn't expecting for the door to be opened and for me to be greeted by the sexiest man I had ever seen in my life. Someone who for some reason I felt I knew. Was it because of the dreams? It seemed more than that. Like I'd been missing a limb until now and here it was.

I swear my heart stopped for a moment.

Something amused him anyway, because Caleb Miller looked at me with a curve upturning the edge of his plump pink lips. He smiled fully, revealing perfect white teeth. He was around six feet tall, and filled out his clothes just right, dressed in a chocolate-brown shirt, and black trousers. His cheekbones were razor sharp and his nose looked like it had been sculpted to perfection. I didn't actually know what to do with myself and when he held out his hand, I was hesitant to take it else I throw myself at him.

Taking a deep breath, I finally shook his hand, coldness seeping through mine. Again, with the cold hands.

"I think your heating system needs work. Everyone here has cold hands." I laughed.

A dark perfect eyebrow arched. "It's the high ceilings and vast rooms. It's a pain to keep warm."

I looked around at the enormous dining hall. "I can imagine. Do you actually eat in here, or is this just for guests?"

"No, I eat here, all alone, every night." It was said with no sorrow, just plain fact. "But we have brought out the best china." He winked. "So, before dinner, would you like a tour of the manor? Then after, we can take a stroll in the gardens. They're well lit, although obviously it won't be as spectacular a view as you'd get during the day."

"Yes, I can imagine it's quite something during the daytime."

He nodded but it seemed strained. Maybe running a rose business wasn't all sweetness and light.

Our walk around the inside of the manor was interesting, but I wasn't one for furniture and ancient artefacts. I liked the living things outside. Our chat was kept polite with my talk about my new surroundings and about the business while Caleb asked me about my own life.

While dinner was served, the conversation took a deeper turn.

"So, our circumstances of meeting are a little,

shall we say, unorthodox. However, do you believe in fate, Vivienne?"

I placed my cutlery on the table. "I do."

"So, tell me the truth of why you came here."

I took a deep exhale, noting that while I did, my breasts rose in my shirt. Caleb's gaze dropped down to them. My heart thudded in response. He picked up a napkin and held it over his mouth, as if dabbing a food stain, but none was there. Maybe he was salivating over me? I would be happy to be dessert. My mind wandered, while I thought about the fact he'd not shown me his bedroom. I wondered if he had a decent sized cock. God would have had to be cruel to give him otherwise.

"Well, you can believe me or not, but I dreamed of here."

He lowered the napkin. "Dreamed? What, you'd seen the business in a magazine and then it had entered your night-time thoughts?"

I shook my head. "No. I dreamed of the rose garden and of a shadowy man in the background. Over and over I dreamed of the roses, painting them when I woke." Leaning down, I opened my folio, extracting one of my paintings. He got up and walked over to me to look, taking the painting from me and placing it on the end of the table.

"Are there more?"

"There are many more, but I brought just five." I took out the other four paintings and placed them on the table, including one similar to that hung above my bed.

"I had never seen this place when I did these," I confessed. "It was on the edge of dreaming and waking that the name Tetburn Manor whispered to me. The next day, I researched Tetburn Manor on the computer and there it was."

"You realise how ludicrous this sounds?" His gaze was serious, burning through me. His eyes like coal.

"You must realise that I'm not a person who cares what I look or sound like. I keep to myself and I paint and I exist, and if I tell you I dreamed of your home, you can believe me or not." I shrugged, looking over the laid out paintings.

"I do believe you."

My head snapped over to him. "You do? Because I have more to tell you."

"As I do you. And when I tell you about myself and Tetburn Manor, you shall realise that I'm not a person who cares what I look or sound like. I keep to myself and I grow roses and if I tell you something about myself it shall be the truth and you can believe me or not."

My own words almost, thrown back at me, adapted for his own use. I smirked. "Intriguing."

We were interrupted by the cook herself bringing dessert. A rich chocolate mousse. The tension in the room was palpable while she placed it in front of us.

"I hope you have enjoyed your meal with us this evening, Miss Gladstone. It has been an honour to serve a new guest."

"The food has been exquisite, thank you," I acknowledged the surprisingly slim woman. Should I have made such delightful food, I'd have been the size of a small house.

"Thank you, Lucinda. That will be all," Caleb said, dismissing her from the room.

"Okay, Sir. Just ring the bell should you require anything later." I noted the quirk to her upper lip as she left us alone.

Silence reigned while his eyes fixed on my mouth as I savoured the flavours and sucked my spoon clean.

I wanted him to push me against the door and push himself inside me.

Caleb sniffed the air and I felt between my brows crease.

"Do you always scent the air like some kind of wolf?"

"Not a wolf." He half-smiled. "But your very essence is intoxicating. Your blood sings to me and your arousal is driving me close to the edge."

My eyes widened at his admission.

He stood and I waited for him to invite me to his bedroom.

"Let's go and see the roses," he said instead.

I hadn't expected such an invitation to actually disappoint me when it came.

Eight

CALEB

She walked into the room and my mind exploded.

My mate.

Mine.

Mine.

Mine.

It took all of my vampire strength to stay still as my nose scented her sweet blood that sang in the air. My hearing detected the rhythmic cadence of her heart beating, and my eyes feasted upon her. Guilt swirled with love and lust creating a kaleidoscope of confusion because at that precise moment, that second of time, my past love faded away. Not due to the years that had passed, but because at the side of this woman before me, my love for Rosemary faded to a black and white photograph, while here in front of me was high definition colour.

Rose tinted cheeks.

Dilated pupils.

Breaths getting deeper.

Heart beating faster.

I kept myself in check throughout the tour of the house, but during dinner the atmosphere of the room thickened. I couldn't take my eyes off the one I knew was the other half of me. The one who completed me.

But there was one huge problem.

She was human.

How could a human woman be my fate?

My mate.

Because I'd made a vow to myself when my last love was slain and I was turned in such a ferocious manner. That I would sire no one.

So how did the woman who now walked next to me as we strolled towards the rose garden fit into my life? Was it to be a passionate love affair that ended when she realised she got older and I did not?

We reached the gate of the garden and I lifted the latch.

I turned to her. "Here we are, but I'm guessing you already know what grows here?"

"A little. The dreams blur a lot of what is here. They show me one rose mainly. It calls to me to come to it. To touch it."

"Show me."

She wandered on the path but as she turned, I already knew where she was going. It was like fate was thoroughly in control and I could not know why, but could only let it take me with it, like a fallen leaf blowing amongst the soil.

The parched ground of the path crunched beneath my feet as she reached the rose of her dreams.

It was called *Rosemary's legacy*. The first rose I had bred. A tribute to my lost love.

And Vivienne had said it called to her in dreams.

She leaned down to it and sniffed the air. "Its fragrance is exactly like in my dreams." She smiled up at me.

"And it asks you to touch it? Why?"

She stood again and sucked in her top lip, bringing her hands back to her sides. "When I touch it, something happens, and then my fate is set. My dreams tell me my present life will end."

"What?" I gasped. "Step away from it. At once," I yelled.

She took a few steps backwards in shock at the vehemence in my voice.

Then her green eyes met mine, amused. "I think it just means figuratively, like a new life starts for me here. How could a rose actually kill me, Caleb?"

"It is not impossible, though improbable. A scratch could get infected and cause sepsis. Sepsis causes organ failure."

"It doesn't scratch me. That's not what happens."

"Then how?"

She lifts up her hand and stares at her thumb.

"A thorn enters my skin, creating a bead of blood. When it drops to the earth that's it. My future is set."

And then I realise the truth. That her blood spilled upon the ground would be too much for my vampire nature. My mate's blood would be no match for my true self. It would command me, and I would become the savage beast I kept in check, claiming my mate with lust and violence.

It was not happening today.

"Let us leave now, and I suggest that for the time being, until I can think upon it more, you don't touch the rose bush."

Her head tilted up towards mine. "You believe me. I've just made the most outlandish claims that sound like I've lost my mind, but you believe me. Why?"

I chose my next words with care. "There's more to this world than most know about. But I think enough has been shared for this evening."

"You said you would tell me about yourself and about Tetburn Manor." Her tone was somewhere between a demand and desperation.

"And I will. But not now. Now I want to show you the rest of the gardens and talk about why I brought you here."

Her eyes clouded with disappointment, but she followed me out of the garden with a last look back at *Rosemary's Legacy*.

"You saw the inside of the manor. It is filled with portrait artwork that to be honest I had given little thought to before. Until I saw you painting. Now the manor feels like it doesn't fit me. There's something disconcerting about the whole thing. It's as if you arrived like a tremor, causing movement to the landscape. I feel awake for the first time in years." I turned and set my eyes upon hers.

"You speak like you are a hundred, not a man of, say, his thirties?"

I smiled. "Is it not rude to speak of someone's age?"

She laughed and it served to unsettle me once again. My tight hold on my emotions was wavering.

"And so you want me to do some paintings for the manor?"

"Yes. I have spoken to Nicholas, the gentleman who actually owns this place and he is happy for the current artwork to be collected and stored and for me to decorate however I choose."

"Ah, so you are a guardian of the manor as opposed to the lord?"

"I am a caretaker of both the manor and of the roses I grow here."

"That you and your family grew here, yes? How long have the Millers been caretakers?"

"Basically since the nineteen-twenties. But we can talk of my history another time. For now, let's talk of what you can create for the manor. It would need to be in keeping with its date."

"I can create printed tapestries maybe, complete

with millefleur. I shall sketch some examples and show you."

"Yes, that would be an idea since I know very little about art. I would also like you to sketch some illustrations for the new rose catalogue if you would. Now, the manor has many rooms, so it is entirely up to you. You can travel here daily, or you may stay here and take a room."

I heard her swallow. Her pause in answering seemed to last hours, not a few seconds. "I'll have to give it some thought. We have only just met after all. Do you not want references? You have seen me camping in your grounds and sneaking out to sketch and paint. I could be a thief or a lunatic."

"And deny our connection?"

Again, I heard her swallow.

"For you dream of here, and I can believe nothing other than this is where you are meant to be. Because my heart beats for you, Vivienne. A sound so loud it threatens to overpower everything I've ever known."

I could resist it no longer. I held her hand and steered her towards a tree near the manor house. She didn't protest. In the shadows, I pushed her back against the bark, and I trailed my fingers from her temple down her cheek. She shivered.

"You're so cold."

"Warm me," I almost growled.

With fervour, I leant down and captured her lips with my own. The warmth from them seemed to seep inside me, heating me where I'd been frozen for so long, melting and thawing my cold, undead heart. Her tongue entered my mouth and I fisted my hands in her hair.

My cock hardened in my pants and I ground myself against her, letting her know just how much of an effect she was having on me.

God, it had been a long, long time since I had felt such emotion, such... passion.

It was only when Vivienne's hand trailed down between us and she stroked my hardness that I jumped back. I could feel my canines descending.

"I'm sorry." I turned away from her. "I shouldn't have done that."

I heard the rustle of material and in my peripheral vision could see her smooth down her clothes.

"Shouldn't you? Are we not destined, Caleb? Do you not feel it? Deny yourself if you will. For now. We both have a lot to consider. I'm going to call for a cab and return home, but I'll be back tomorrow, you can bet on that. Tomorrow I will be here again and this time I shall sit amongst the roses of the garden and see whether the whispers of my dreams become screams in reality."

"Until tomorrow," I replied, still turned away from her, and then I walked away, because if I did anything else she would see my true nature and I wasn't ready to reveal myself just yet.

Nine

VIVIENNE

I slumped upon my bed, my mind whirling as it replayed our conversations and recounted every minute of my evening spent at Tetburn Manor. Was it the roses that called me, or was it their mysterious breeder? I had wanted him, craved him between my thighs and now I was unsatisfied.

Nearly a whole bottle of wine later, I felt no better and the cravings started again. I pulled my robe tighter about myself and rocked on the sofa.

No. No. NO.

I will not answer your call.

But then I was on my feet as if someone else had

stood me there and I walked into the bathroom, opened the cabinet and took out a fresh blade.

I stared at it and closed my eyes.

Imagine it's the scratch of a rose bush.

As the garden of Tetburn Manor flashed vividly in my mind, I threw the blade into the bin under the sink. Climbing into bed with a pad and pencils, I sketched over and over until my mind quieted and I fell into a fitful sleep.

Touch me.

Love me.

Feel me.

Let me.

I dreamed of calling voices and of razorblades slashing across my throat. I saw myself lying on the floor in a pool of red, my eyes wide open and staring. I gasped one word.

'Caleb'.

The next morning it took four cups of coffee and an almost cold shower before I felt anywhere near in a state to travel. I dressed as I felt in a black t-shirt and black jeans. I felt a day of charcoal ahead of me and almost took the coloured paints from my backpack, only to leave them in there at the last minute.

The sun shone down on Tetburn Manor and the closer I got, the more my mood improved. It was strange to be walking once again down the West Bridge.

A man met me, introducing himself as Jenson. Tall and burly, he said he mainly did security for the manor, but that Caleb had asked him to pass me a wicker basket.

I smiled, as this macho man looked ridiculous holding a wicker basket with a yellow gingham ribbon on it.

"Thank you. Am I okay to go through to the garden? I'll be working there."

"Yes, Miss Gladstone. If you need to come inside to use the facilities, then please press the buzzer as there are not many people around this morning. I'll make sure one of the security team lets you in and shows you the way."

"That's okay, I saw where they were last night."

His eyes burned into mine. "We'll still need to escort you."

I shrugged. Whatever made this guy feel superior.

"So, where's Caleb?" I asked him.

"If Mr Miller wished for you to know his current business, you'd already know it," he said curtly. "As I said, please buzz if you need anything." With that he turned and walked away.

"Okay then." I mumbled to myself and I went to the garden.

I decided that today I would just sit on the bench outside of it as I had in my dreams and I would sketch it from there. Setting up my easel, I wondered where Caleb was. I was disappointed he hadn't come to say hello, seeing as I was here on his personal invite. I remembered the hamper I'd put down earlier and I reached down flipping open the lids. Inside I found croissants, jam, a knife, a small bottle of orange juice and one of water. There was a can of cold coffee, an apple, an orange, and a slice of what appeared to be Madeira cake. A note inside said:

Sorry, I can't be there to deliver this myself.
I will be around at four should you still be here.

Ten

CALEB

I sighed. I wasn't sure I still would be around. The sun was scorching and even with breaks in the shade, if I wasn't able to even piss without security then I'm sure I wouldn't be able to sit in the drawing room for a rest. Maybe I should take the room Caleb offered? Just for a few days until my preliminary sketches were drawn.

Yeah, that's why you want to stay. You tell yourself that.

The next day I deliberately didn't turn up to sketch until two o'clock in the afternoon. Once more, I stayed outside of the garden, adding more depth to the work I did the day before. As it passed four pm, I started to glance at the house waiting for Caleb to appear, feeling my body tense when he didn't.

And then Jenson was there again in front of me.

"Mr Miller wishes to know if you'd like to join him for refreshments and to discuss the sketches you have made so far?"

I nodded and walking past Jenson's stern and watchful face, I made my way back into the manor house.

Daria greeted me, a firm smile on her face. "He's in the drawing room today, first door on your left." I followed where her outstretched fingers were pointing.

The room I walked into took my breath away. It was light and airy, with cream walls. Pale-blue heavy drapes hung at the windows, their exact shade matched with the two sofas in the room. Cream carpets had me leaving my shoes at the doorway. Air conditioning whirred in the background and it had the smell of not having been switched on for a while. I wrinkled my nose and walked over to the windows feeling the depth of the luxury pile around my feet. "Why not let some fresh air in?"

Caleb was behind me in a second. In fact, I didn't quite know how he could have reached my side so quickly. I must have been distracted. He pulled my hands away from the window catches.

"Flies get in. They drive me crazy. So I'd rather put up with the AC."

He was so close to me, and he hadn't taken his hands off mine.

Turning around, I stared at him. Leaning toward him I lifted onto my tiptoes and brushed my lips against his own.

My breath hitched at our closeness and I listened to see if he was reacting the same way.

I didn't hear his breath.

Shaking my head, I leaned closer once more and again rested my lips against his. I waited to feel his breath escape his mouth and move over my lips.

There was nothing.

I stepped back and stared at him.

"Why can't I tell you're breathing? How are you doing that? It can't be good to hold your breath for that long."

Caleb stayed close to me and spoke softly. "I'm not holding my breath. It's one of the things I need to tell you about myself. Just as you were surprised that you made what you said in your own words were 'outlandish claims', well I have my own to make. The first is that I don't breathe."

I raised my brows. "Don't be ridiculous, everyone needs to breathe, or you'd die."

"I'm already dead." His eyes stared into mine. We were but inches apart.

"Have you taken some drugs, Caleb? Because I'm finding this conversation extremely confusing. You aren't making sense. What's the point to this?"

"The point is I said I would tell you about myself, and I am. I don't breathe because I'm not alive."

I backed away from him. "Caleb, this isn't funny. Now stop these silly games and let's talk about my sketches. I was going to tell you I'd decided to stay here, but now I'm not sure you are safe to be around. I have my own mental health issues. I can't cope with someone else's right now."

"Vivienne." He pulled me closer, his hands moving to the small of my back. His cold fingers were against my bare skin under my t-shirt. "Look at me."

I did. I looked up into those hypnotizing browns

and waited for words to come from those pillow-soft lips.

"I'm a vampire."

I went to pull away, but I didn't move even a millimetre. I tried to move again but I was held in a grasp as secure as a tightened straitjacket.

"What the...?"

"Think about it. My hands are cold as ice. I don't breathe. You don't see me in the daytime. My strength is such that you can't move me. My speed is such that I was at your side before you could open a window, and the reason I didn't want you to is because there is still sunlight outside and if that touches my skin I will burn. The windows have a protective cover."

"I don't believe you. You say you're dead, but your heart beats."

"My heart started beating the same day you first came to Tetburn Manor. Before that it stopped beating when I was turned. Vampire lore states that a vampire's heart will beat again when they meet their mate. You are my mate, Vivienne. You are my one. My heart beats for you."

There was a clatter, and we sprang apart and turned watching as Daria began picking up pieces of the tea set she had been carrying in.

"My apologies. I am so sorry to disturb you both. I was just bringing in some refreshments and I was startled at your declaration, Sir. Are you sure Vivienne is the one?"

He nodded. "I am, Daria. You can leave the spillages, for Vivienne and I must talk further. I will call you later."

"Yes, Sir." Daria nodded leaving the room quickly. Too quickly.

"Is Daria...?"

"Yes. About 60% of the staff are vampires, the rest are human. The humans work security as we need that 24-hours and also they work in the rose business."

He gestured towards the sofa and I took a seat. "Are you beginning to believe me?"

"I don't know what to think," I said truthfully. "None of what has been happening to me lately makes sense and part of me feels that maybe my own mind has finally broken and that's what I'm experiencing now."

"Then I shall show you that you are really here and really experiencing things," Caleb said.

He moved onto the couch and leaning over, his lips met mine once more. And then I didn't care whether I was hallucinating, or he was lying. I just wanted his body on me, in me, everywhere.

He opened his mouth and licked his tongue over his teeth, and I gasped as his canines descended. His brown eyes took on a russet shade as red danced with the browns. I reached out a hand and he clasped my wrist with his firm grip guiding my fingers up to his mouth. The index and middle finger of my right hand entered his mouth and touched a canine. It seemed more intimate than sex itself in that moment as I felt at the sharp tooth. He pulled my finger away before I could press on too firmly.

Then his mouth was back on mine. I could tell by the tautness of his body that he was keeping himself in check with me. But then again, I was a delicate human, and he was... my mind pondered it... a vampire.

The idea that vampires existed was ludicrous, but somehow, I knew that's what Caleb was. His body was cold against mine and yet it set off a fire within me that threatened to engulf my whole being.

He helped me out of my clothes and stripped out of his and then he was on top of me, his fingers stroking at my wet core, while his mouth trailed down my neck. I wondered if he would bite me like I'd seen in films.

And then he was pushing inside me and I wrapped my legs around him. Despite the strength he'd shown me, he fucked me like any human man, except I could tell there was an extra depth of passion, of ardour.

His orgasm chased mine and we trembled together and then rested in each other's arms. He stroked my face as we laid together. But although I'd come, I was unsatisfied. I wanted the whole of him and he'd given me only a piece.

I just had to hope that this was the start of something more.

Eleven

CALEB

I needed her.

She consumed my thoughts and taking her body had made things worse not better. I craved her. For the next few days I kept my distance as my blood thirst was so high. I felt I would surely kill her if she came near my arms.

I watched her on the security camera footage. Saw the hurt in her eyes as she gazed at the manor. Saw her sketch like a crazy person. Saw her leave.

Her eyes lost their sparkle.

Their shine dulled.

Shadows returned to her face, to the underneath of her eyes.

She wore long sleeved hooded tops on a warm day and the foolish man I am thought she was doing it to protect her skin from the sun.

Until her sleeve fell down while sketching and my vampire vision homed in on the scratches on her skin.

She was still outside when I rose the next day. The weather was dull and so I left the manor and stomped over to where she sat on the stone bench.

"Show me your arms." I snarled.

Her head turned to me slowly, eyes dead, and she shook her head. "No. My body is my business. I offered it to you days ago and you took it and then you threw me away."

My teeth ground together in my mouth. "I did not throw *you* away. I kept *myself* away, because I am dangerous. Do you know what I can do to you?"

She held up her arm and let a sleeve drop down slightly showing scabbed cuts and scars of past harm. "Is it any more than what I do to myself?"

"Yes, it's more." Walking over, I grabbed her and ripped the sleeve straight off her top like it was made of tissue paper. It revealed her whole arm, the tracks of silvery scars, some thicker than others, and the new scratches. "These scratches are like a chaste kiss from me. My cuts run deep."

She pulled her arm back to herself and I let her.

"My own run deep on occasion," she scoffed at me. "But for some reason I always survive. Yet now here I am, called to be the mate of a vampire. Do you really believe I'm supposed to stay human?"

"I won't turn you, Vivienne. My mate or not, we shall stay vampire and his human love. There will be no immortal bite."

Bitterness twisted at her features.

"Leave me alone, Caleb. I want to finish my sketch in peace."

"You said you would move in," I reminded her.

"That was before you rejected me."

My voice rose. "I am not rejecting you. I am protecting you."

"Then return to your manor and let me draw." She picked up her pencils and turned away from me.

"I'm inside if you want to join me for dinner," I told her. Then I began to make my way back to the manor. I needed time to think. What was I supposed to do? She was clearly suffering, but I had no idea of our destiny.

I hadn't even reached the front door when I found out that Vivienne knew exactly what our destiny was. As I heard the gate swing shut, I realised where she was headed.

I flew into the rose garden, reaching Vivienne's side as she leaned down. I heard her short gasp as the thorn pierced her skin.

She lifted up her thumb and we watched as she took out the thorn and the crimson bead bloomed on her flesh, before dropping onto the ground. Her eyes caught mine just as the scent of her blood hit my nose and then she was in my arms and we were speeding up to my room. I didn't know what was next, but I knew she had indeed set fate in motion and that what happened from here was not in either of our control.

I threw her on the bed. I was not gentle this time, although I wasn't at full strength either. She bounced on the covers and scrambled to sit up.

Her eyes widened as she saw me and I knew what she was taking in. My eyes would be vivid red with blood lust, my fangs sharp.

The blood from her thumb had continued to run down her hand and I launched myself, now naked, onto the bed. I licked her thumb, swiping my tongue over the tiny cut and sealing it closed with my vampire saliva, and then I cleansed her hand of the drying blood. Her essence fizzed and sparked in my mouth and my mind.

Mine.

Mine.

Mine.

My mate.

I tore her clothes from her body and when she lay there bare before me and panting, I looked at her closely and saw no fear, just sheer unbridled lust.

I moved over her and this time I had no intention of being gentle.

I bit and nipped at her body. It might cause small bruises, love-bites, but I hadn't broken skin. She gasped and writhed in my arms. I thrust deep inside her, fucking her hard and fast, and at the point of our completion I bit down on her neck and let her blood flow into my mouth.

She screamed as her orgasm shook her body.

Her heartbeat sang in my ears and as I heard it slow, I withdrew my fangs, licked over the marks to heal them and gathered her in my arms.

"This is all I can offer you right now. I offer you me. The man and the monster. I can't offer you immortality."

Vivienne looked up at me sleepy and sated. "Maybe this is enough," she said, before closing her eyes.

Vivienne moved into the manor taking a guest room down the hall from mine that Daria had prepared. In the daytime, she sketched and painted. Sometimes she took picnics to the nearby lake. In the evenings we dined together and then we would retire to my room where we would make love or fuck hard. Once she fell asleep in my arms, I'd transfer her to her own room and then I'd work before the dawn rose and my own slumber called.

But as days turned into weeks, I saw the paleness of my mate's skin. She became tired and I feared she was anaemic. I stopped my bite and as her colour returned to her cheeks, it faded from her existence. Her paintings got darker. Her smiles became fewer. I knew what would happen next, and I waited for the conversation I didn't want to take place.

"I need you to turn me, Caleb. I told you my dream. It said Tetburn Manor would be where I began, ended, and began again. You know what that means." Her voice rose as she snarled near my face, so close a tiny bit of spittle hit my cheek.

"Your dreams did not specify you would die. And dreams are exactly that anyway. Dreams. Fragments of your imagination playing in your brain."

Her eyes darkened. It was like her soul leached out as we spoke. I needed to get her painting again.

Painting and the rose garden brought the light to her eyes.

"I had Daria help me turn one of the rooms into an artist's studio. I don't know why I hadn't thought of it before. Come look." I took her hand and dragged her to the room next to her own. Pushing it open, she walked in, taking in the plain white walls and the plain canvasses everywhere. A white unit held every paint and brush she could ever desire.

"This room looks out over the front of the house. You could paint the bridge, the new meadow. Now even on a rainy day, you can do that which makes you happiest."

"Thank you, Caleb," she said, smiling at me.

But her words rang out hollow like the empty echoes of the room we stood in, and she looked around the room as if it sealed her fate to the blankness of her current existence.

Twelve

VIVIENNE

He said he wanted me.

I knew his heart fought his head.

His head was winning.

While I lost.

I was so goddamn tired. All my emotions were leached out onto the canvasses I painted. My heavy heart was a burden to carry.

Now Caleb would take me to his bed, but he wouldn't take blood from me. Not anymore. He kept the main part of himself—the vampire, his true nature—from me, and he expected me to accept that.

He left me no choice, because I would rather

have his company than none of him at all, but it hurt. It hurt so much. Life hurt, living hurt. But I knew I'd been here before in the dark recesses of my mind, and I'd fought through and won. I would find the light, the colours, and I would live with my immortal beloved until...

It was a question I had no answer for.

Until...

I'd been painting. I'd enjoyed an early evening dinner with Caleb and then I'd come out to the stone bench to sketch the rose garden while he held business meetings. I would see him tomorrow. Tonight, he was busy until past my own bedtime. I felt so aristocratic this evening, dressed in a white cotton summer dress, a picnic hamper containing strawberries and champagne at my feet. It was the last thing I remembered. Tasting the sweetness and savouring its fizz on my tongue.

And now? Now I woke, my head banging. As I opened my eyes, I could make out that I was tied to a chair back in my new art studio. How the fuck had I got here?

I looked around me, at my white studio, and

then fragments of a dream rose and tangled with the reality of my current life.

"Who are you?" the voice had come from behind me. From behind the stone bench.

I turned around. "I'm Vivienne." I was confused. They knew my name.

"Yes, but **who are you***? As in why are you here? Why do you keep visiting my manor, my garden?"*

Their manor. What were they talking about?

"I don't know. I just need to be here."

"But why?"

"Because it's the only place I feel alive."

Then I saw them sitting staring at me, and I knew.

"But you don't feel alive at the manor do you, Vivienne? Not anymore. It's death you seek now, or rather un-death. But your being there is changing things. Things that have been as they are for years. I don't want you here. You're getting in the way of my own plans."

My death was imminent. I didn't know what I'd been given, but I kept nodding off and waking again.

The skin on my arms was ripped open. This time I did not welcome the pain. A gag around my mouth stifled my screams and as I slowly bled, they smiled. They took me off the chair and laid me on the floor on a massive canvas. My mouth gagged, and my wrists and ankles bound, I laid there as the blood dripped out of me creating its own work of art. I began to lose consciousness once more.

The dream moved on and I was standing inside the manor in a room with bare white walls. Yet, instead of feeling the peace I got from Tetburn, here my heart was gripped with fear as I turned around and around, seeing nothing but the white.

And then there was pain.

I most certainly was not numb here.

My captor stood watching.

The pain at my throat was excruciating and bright red blood sprayed out and coated the bare white wall in front of me.

I looked down at my white gown. It looked like I'd spilled red wine, but I knew it wasn't wine at all.

The door clicked closed and I laid there, my life ebbing away, and then I saw her. She knelt beside me, her long red hair soft around her face. I knew who she was. Rosemary. A ghost from the past.

"It's almost time," she whispered.

Thirteen

CALEB

"Have you seen Vivienne?" I asked Jenson as I returned from the grounds where she'd told me she would be painting, my meeting having been cancelled.

"No, Sir. But that's strange as I haven't seen Daria this evening either. Maybe they went somewhere together?"

"I doubt it. Daria rarely goes anywhere. I bet Vivienne is in her room or the studio."

"Sir, this may be me speaking out of turn, but lately Daria has been acting a little oddly, saying things like that the routine of the manor is changing, and well, you were aware of her feelings for you, weren't you?"

I stood stock still staring at my security manager. "Daria... has feelings for me? You must be mistaken."

He looked at me like you might stare at someone who'd just been found wandering dazed. "She's in love with you. Has been for years."

My mind refused to believe his words. Surely, he was wrong?

"I'll go check Vivienne's rooms. Can you be checking the cameras?"

"Certainly, Sir."

I ran up the stairs but as I reached the top, I stopped, sucker punched as the smell of my mate's blood hung in the air. I knew the blood was leaving her body, there was too much. Had she delivered the final cuts to herself that would take her from me, from this life? How could I have been so stupid to not turn her and make her my own? Then we could have lived together forever. Now I might face another great loss in my life.

Stupid.

Stupid.

Stupid.

But as I flung open the door, instead I saw Daria

leaning over the body of Vivienne, blood dripping from her mouth.

I took a stroll in the park, Rosemary's arm in mine.

"It's such a beautiful evening," she said, staring at the moonlit sky.

"Every evening I'm with you is a beautiful evening," I told her.

She smiled at me, the light of the moon catching in her eyes, and I was full of love for her, and then she was no longer there.

I heard then saw her body hit the tree and I watched as a tall, pale-skinned man with dark hair ripped out her throat in front of my eyes.

He looked up at me, his own eyes blazing red, and he laughed.

And then he came for me...

As blood lust hit and my true vampire nature took over, I picked up Daria and threw her against the wall. As an immortal like myself I'd only be able to kill her by stake and right now I needed to get to Vivienne. If she came at me again, I'd throw her clean through the window.

"Caleb, *stop*, I was licking her wounds closed," Daria gasped. "Look at her if you don't believe me. Look at the canvas. She had blood draining out everywhere. You need to turn her, quickly. She's too weak to survive."

Staring down at the body of my mate, I saw that Daria's words were true. The wound on her neck was almost closed.

I turned to her. "So, if you didn't do this, who?"

"I don't know. Jenson said he'd heard Vivienne scream. I came to look."

"Jenson," I roared, realising who the true betrayer was though I knew not why.

"He left her bleeding profusely and sent you thinking you would kill her," I realised.

"Well luckily, I wasn't hungry, because my lover and I had just partaken of each other."

"Your lover?"

"Lucinda."

Lucinda? The cook? How could I have not known?

Clearly my question was painted across my features.

"I have always kept my own affairs from you, Sir, as I'd felt it wouldn't be right, not when you mourned your past love so deeply," Daria explained.

"Ah." I'd been too lost in my own world to see my house manager and cook were in love. I was a selfish man.

"I shall go take care of Jenson. He cannot have

got far." Daria's eyes flashed deep red and I saw the monster awaken within her.

"No. He will be prepared. He could kill you."

"Let us not forget I am a vampire, Sir. I have met many a human male who has underestimated me."

Then the window was open, and she was gone.

I looked down at the woman in my arms. Her heart was thready and weak, her pallor pale, and her breathing shallow. She was unconscious and I now had a choice. I could take her to the nearest A&E Department and leave her there. I could visit her and use compulsion to wipe her mind of ever having known me. Or I could turn her.

As I gazed at her face, her mouth opened, and she spoke.

"She is your destiny, Caleb. You need to live. Let *all* the roses go."

As I gasped at hearing my past love's voice come from the mouth of my present, Vivienne's body slumped, and I knew there was no time left and my decision was made.

I drained her to the point of death and then tore open my wrist with my teeth. As the blood pooled there, I held my wrist below her mouth and let drops of blood fall between her lips. A minute later, her eyes opened, a red sheen over her emerald gaze like the scorching of grass. Then she began to lap, her mouth fixing on my wrist as she sucked. My cock hardened as she drank from me. Euphoria sang in my veins as she fed, but she would be too weak for anything else. My fledgling, my eternal lover. The immortal bite had taken place and now we would be together for as long as fate allowed. I gathered her in my arms and her eyes closed as she sighed with satiation. The next few nights would be brutal for her as she made the change, but I would be with her every step of the way.

Fourteen

VIVIENNE

Rosemary showed me a vision.

I stood in a cemetery as a seventeen-year-old. On the cusp of adulthood, the illness that had taken my mother's life was fully taking root in mine. My father told us to take a flower each and throw it on top of the coffin. He'd ordered lilies. Our mother's favourite flowers were roses. I stepped away to a rose bush planted next to a nearby grave and I pulled the head off the flower.

Walking back, I scowled at my father and my brother and sister in turn and then I threw the petals over my mother's sunken coffin.

I knew now that the rose I'd picked had been 'Rosemary's legacy'. Planted there years before by a man who'd lost his wife, his Rose, and had ordered a bush from Tetburn in commemoration.

It was another piece of the puzzle that had brought me to Tetburn Manor.

"I followed all my roses," Rosemary whispered to me as I laid there in my white dress in a pool of red. Jenson had slashed at my skin so many times. Was Rosemary here to take me with her? "And this one, near your mother's grave, led me to you. You struggled to live in life, but you will blossom in your rebirth."

I stared at her. What did she mean?

"Take care of him," she said. "I can leave now. Be happy. Forget the roses."

The door opened and the shadow man was there. I could feel his presence.

I turned around and I saw his teeth.

Large incisors as white as the walls.

And I saw his eyes.

As red as the blood spraying from my throat.

And I heard his heart beating.

Th-thud.

Th-thud.

Th-thud.

As I knew my own was ceasing.

I lost consciousness then and when I awoke, I found myself in loving arms, with a violent thirst for blood.

Days passed.

A hunger like I had never known.

They fed me: Caleb, Daria, and another woman. They brought me blood. So much blood.

I was in Caleb's room, and one day, I opened my eyes and the raging thirst was past. Rather than be desperate for blood, I was desperate for my love.

He stood up from a chair at the side of our bed.

"How are you feeling?"

I closed my eyes and stretched out my limbs.

I felt *strong*.

Smiling at my love, I pulled back the bedcovers.

"I feel hungry, Caleb... for *you*."

This time we didn't have to hold back, either of us. We nipped and fed from each other. Caleb pushed inside of me hard. We were a tangle of limbs, hitting the floor, the walls, as we reached dizzy new heights.

I might have quenched my immediate thirst for

blood, but my thirst for Caleb would last several lifetimes.

Fifteen

VIVIENNE

Jenson had resented his legacy of having to serve the undead; the fact it was instilled upon him by his parents that he had to serve someone he felt not worthy. He'd asked Daria why immortality meant manor houses and being human meant servitude. It was a blinkered, small-minded attitude, but then he'd seen nothing much of the real world, his existence largely limited to manor life and vows of silence about the truth of who owned and worked at Tetburn Manor.

Caleb's obsession with his roses and trust in his staff had meant he was unaware of Jenson watching on his security monitors as he tapped into his bank accounts. Unaware that while he slept, Jenson had installed spyware that watched what keys he clicked. Money that was being siphoned off into a private account, ready for him to make his escape.

But he'd panicked at my arrival. At the manor routine changing. At Caleb becoming more aware of his surroundings.

His plan had been to turn us on ourselves, to get us to destroy each other and then stake whoever remained. He was in charge of security. There would have been no evidence left. Then he would have been free to do as he pleased, he'd told Daria, as she'd hung him on a rusty hook to encourage his confession.

He'd become greedy, making a plan with some other staff to continue on as if Caleb were still alive and to sell as much of the manor and its roses as possible and then disappear with the profits.

Daria had dropped him off with Nicholas after learning of the other staffs involvement and then she returned to the manor, her and Lucinda helping Caleb to care for me until I'd gotten past my fledgling stage. They'd become good friends.

My new undead life was mesmerising. Colours were vivid, tastes exquisite, smells delectable. I was hypnotised by life. But I no longer wanted to paint it. The feeling had left me. Now I wanted to experience it all. To travel the world and see everything with my new senses. I wanted to see it all with Caleb. My mate, my lover. We could now be free with each other, love and make love without restraint. Touch was electric. Feelings in overload. My happiness knew no bounds.

Caleb had wondered what to do about his and Rosemary's legacy of roses until one afternoon we found a blight had hit them all. Every one was black and withered, even the yellow one. It was just as I'd seen in my dreams.

The blight was unidentifiable, but I knew what it was.

Rosemary's final message.

Nicholas was taking the house back, landscaping the grounds and turning the place into an art gallery, among which would be some of my own paintings of the house and the gardens. The roses would live on, but not in a way that required constant tending.

And so we could come back to visit them whenever we liked. But for now, myself, Caleb, Daria, and Lucinda were leaving Tetburn Manor. We were going to travel. We didn't know where we would end up, just that we intended to see as much of the beauty of life as we could.

Caleb took my arm and we turned to walk out across the West Bridge for the final time. "You look as beautiful as ever, my mate."

My arms bore no scars. Everything had healed, borne new, as I also became new.

Life's bite had been far more dangerous than the immortal one.

Now I knew peace and I welcomed it.

THE END

I hope you enjoyed this novella. For more like this, pre-order my dark and twisted paranormal fairy tale retelling CAGING ELLA for the introductory first in series price of just 0.99:
books2read.com/u/3RzZXB
(out June 2023)

Continue on to read the playlist for Immortal Bite and the description and a sneak peek of Caging Ella.

For more on my paranormal romcom, join my mailing list and receive the short story prequel to **The Supernatural Dating Agency** series, *Dating Sucks*:

geni.us/andiemlongparanormal

Playlist

I rarely have a playlist, but Caleb and Vivienne's love story was enhanced by playing some inspirational, dark, and 'feels' hitting songs. Thank you to the following artists and the songwriters etc behind them.

Running Up That Hill. *Placebo.*
For You. *Liam Payne & Rita Ora.*
Never Enough. *Loren Allred.*
Surrender. *Paloma Faith.*
Bleeding Love. *Leona Lewis.*
Born to Die. *Lana Del Rey.*

Caging Ella

SUMMARY

A paranormal fairy tale re-telling... of vampires, captivity, and love.

They said that *Once Upon a Time*, Cinderella resided with her monstrous stepmother, ugly stepsisters, and led a life of cruel drudgery, until one day, a fairy godmother helped her attend a ball, where she met a charming prince and lived happily ever after.

But what if he was a dark prince? A vampire? And Ella the daughter of his maid? What if he wanted Ella to birth his children? Could not wait for a taste of her sweet chaste desire...

After six years of captivity with her cruel father and stepfamily, will Ella wish to be free, or will she tie herself to Beau for eternity?

SNEAK PEEK

He arched a brow. "You think hook-ups are risqué?"

"No, I just hope you have condoms. Because either you get a disease, or you get a child you treat as a disease. Better the potential ends up in a litter bin."

"You are very bitter for one so young."

"And you are very strange for whatever age you are."

He laughed then. "You're right. I am. I am very strange. And I won't be screaming in passion in the park because I am actually saving my seed for the right person to carry my children. Can you believe that? When you look upon me, do I seem like someone who would want to do things right?"

Who spoke like this? And why was I carrying on a conversation with a weirdo I should have told to go away by now? There was just something about him. Maybe the fact he was letting me have an opinion. Was listening to me. Dismissing my thoughts, I shrugged. "People show their true faces and still you can't tell the monsters from the good guys," I said. "When I look upon you, I cannot decide whether you are a psychopath playing with me before you murder me, someone bored who is amusing themselves at my expense, or someone in need of a straitjacket."

"I'll give you a clue. I'm kind of all three."

"And what do you see, when you look upon me?" I asked him, because as weird as this evening had gotten, he was distracting me from my grief, albeit temporarily.

"Hmmm." He looked me up and down but stared far longer at my face than my body. "I see someone who life has made hard as stone. There's a crack there with light trying to seep out, but here you are in the darkness, resisting letting it break further open."

"I think I'd like to be alone again now," I said dismissively, because he was too close to the truth.

About Andie

Andie M. Long lives in Sheffield, UK, with her long-suffering partner, her son, and a gorgeous Whippet furbaby. She's addicted to coffee and Toblerone.

When not being partner, mother, or writer, she can usually be found wasting far too much time watching TikTok.

Andie's Reader Group on Facebook

https://www.facebook.com/groups/haloandhornshangout

TikTok and Instagram
@andieandangelbooks

Paranormal Romance By
Andie

SUPERNATURAL DATING AGENCY

The Vampire wants a Wife
A Devil of a Date
Hate, Date, or Mate
Here for the Seer
Didn't Sea it Coming
Phwoar and Peace

Also on audio and in paperback.

THE PARANORMALS

Hex Factor
Heavy Souls

We Wolf Rock You
Satyrday Night Fever

Also in paperback. Complete series ebook available.

Sucking Dead

Suck My Life – available on audio.
My Vampire Boyfriend Sucks
Sucking Hell
Suck it Up
Hot as Suck
Just My Suck
Too Many Sucks

Paranormal Fairy Tale Re-Tellings

Filthy Rich Vampires – Reverse Harem
Royal Rebellion (Last Rites/First Rules duet) –
Time Travel Young Adult Fantasy
Immortal Bite – Gothic romance